Luidibalthaz and the Widufulka

A Collection of Moral Tales for Storytelling

ISBN: 9798378878505

I dedicate this book to my son for whom I wrote these stories as a way to pass on my ideals to him and, gods willing, to any others who may read these words whether I reside here or in the halls of the hereafter.

Foreword

As I stated in my dedication, I wrote these stories to pass along lessons which I found important to my child. The choice of a Germanic theme was only because of my own linguistic preference, our predominant heritage, and my own faith choice. I do not profess to be an intellectual leader in the field of Germanic studies or linguistics, there are many out there far more qualified who have put forth many studious years toward that goal, and I do not profess that these stories are in any way historical. These stories are entirely the creation of my mind.

That having been said, I did take inspiration from oral storytelling traditions, especially that of "Bronze Age" (a very loose and Eurocentric term, but one that fits stylistically in this case) hero traditions. I tried to use fairly repetitive techniques to help with memorizing the gist of stories so that they may be told with individual embellishment or edition.

I encourage these stories to be told around campfires, in dim lights, under stars, with great animation and movement. Let your audience enjoy the exciting sort of stories that inspired novels, plays, radio dramas, and films that stories have evolved into over the millenia.

-Matthew Wilson

Saiwif and Skeujamann

Long ago, in ancient woods, there were two beings, wights of nature, that roamed among the trees and animals.

One of the wights stayed to her path, steady and calm; while the other flew through the branches of the trees, this way and that, with little care to whatever else may be about.

They were Saiwif, a wight of water, and Skeujamann, a wight of wind.

Skeujamann would fly about in fits and stalls, shaking the branches of the trees and taunting Saiwif, pestering her about the limits of her path and flaunting the freedom of his movement.

Saiwif would quietly listen to Skeujamann's boasts, ignoring him.

This only made Skeujamann more determined to pester her. After many days of this Saiwif began losing her temper and her waters became a tempest whenever Skeujamann flew about her, the waves breaking on the shores of her banks and beaches and washing away land, trees, and animals.

This continued on for many days until the creatures of the woods cried out to the gods and Wodanaz descended to help them.

Wodanaz heard them and chose two wise, but mischievous, creatures to help Him; a pair of ravens named Sehwan and Hlusin.

Wodanaz disguised Himself as an old man and walked into the woods while Sehwan and Hlusin flew out to find Skeujamann and Saiwif.

Sehwan found Skeujamann and watched him shake the branches of the trees, scare the animals, and taunt Saiwif with his antics.

Hlusin perched upon a treebranch and listened to Saiwif rage about the taunts and boasts of Skeujamann.

Sehwan and Hlusin both flew back to Wodanaz and told him what they saw and heard.

Sehwan said, "Wodanaz, Skeujamann flies about, shakes the branches, and boasts; but he does not have anyone to share his antics with nor to temper his fits."

Hlusin said, "Wodanaz, Saiwif is filled with anger at Skeujamann but her anger is filled with hurt of being trapped within her shores and banks while he flies about freely."

Wodanaz listened to the two ravens and thought carefully, then said, "Sehwan, fly to Skeujamann and taunt him and make him chase you to me. Hlusin, fly to Saiwif and ask her of her troubles, then sit and listen to her quietly until another comes."

The ravens did as Wodanaz bade them.

Sehwan boasted of his graceful flight and beautiful feathers until Skeujamann chased him through the trees to Wodanaz.

Skeujamann did not recognize Wodanaz, since He was disguised as an old man, and the wind spirit blew at Him with all his force.

Not even a thread on Wodanaz's tunic moved. Skeujamann blew and blew and blew, but still not even a single thread of Wodanaz's tunic moved. Skeujamann tired and laid down on the mossy floor of the woods in front of Wodanaz.

Wodanaz sat down beside him and asked, "Is it not tiring to blow about these woods alone?"

Skeujamann responded sadly, "No one will join me in my games and jests, so I must do them all alone."

Wodanaz gently held the wind spirit, saying, "But do you not think about others' feelings? How do you think Saiwif feels about your jesting and flying about?"

Skeujamann began to cry and said, "But she moves rocks and trees and other things! She is filled with fish and frogs and beasts! She reflects the sun and the moon and the stars! She is beautiful while no one sees me unless I shake the trees! How can she be saddened by me?"

Wodanaz smiled and asked Ingwaz to make a great dark cloud in the sky. He said, "Carry this to her, then ask her and listen."

Skeujamann carried the cloud to Saiwif, who had calmed as she spoke to Hlusin. The cloud burst with rain, feeding her, and Skeujamann and Saiwif spoke on and on.

Their friendship and love grew stronger as time went on and Skeujamann still brings rains to and from Saiwif to this day and listens to her stories.

The Wights and the Widufulka

Saiwif and Skeujamann spent many years telling
each other tales and watching over the beasts of
the woods and the fish of the streams and lakes.
One day new beasts wandered into the woods.
These beasts wore skins and cloths and walked
upon two legs. These beasts were fulka. Saiwif and
Skeujamann watched these new beasts warily and
were greatly upset when the fulka picked the
berries that the deer ate, used the branches of the
trees to hunt the deer and other beasts, and caught
the fish from the streams and lakes.
Skeujamann then made great gusts of wind to
scare the new fulka away.
Saiwif then made great waves in her streams and
lakes to scare the new fulka away.
The fulka were scared and ready to move away
when Wodanaz, and his wife Frijjo, appeared to
them and comforted them.

Saiwif and Skeujamann went to the gods and exclaimed, "But these fulka eat the food of our beasts! These fulka kill and eat our beasts from both wood and stream and lake!"

Wodanaz replied, "I have led these fulka here, and here is where they shall live."

Saiwif and Skeujamann then became angry and a storm grew about them, "What can these fulka have that our beasts and trees do not?!"

Frijjo replied, "You shall discover that for yourselves." She then turned the wights into fulka. Skeujamann and Saiwif were then alone in the wood with not even a garment upon their backs. Skeujamann and Saiwif wept and wept for they were afraid and without their powers. A young fulka woman, Ermunahildiz, then found them and asked, "Who are you to be alone in these woods?" Skeujamann and Saiwif only wept and wept. Ermunahildiz brought more fulka to them and they gave them clothing and food. Skeujamann and Saiwif went with the fulka and discovered the art and music and love that fulka shared among each other. They were welcomed among the fulka and Skeujamann and Saiwif had a child, the first of the fulka to be born in the woods, named Luidibalþaz. Skeujamann and Saiwif taught the fulka of the land and winds and waters.

Skeujamann and Saiwif grew to love the fulka and named them the Widufulka, welcoming them into their woods. When Luidibalþaz came of age, Skeujamann and Saiwif were changed back into wights of the wind and water, having grown to love the new fulka of their land.

Thus are fulka to this day responsible for the land and water that they have been granted stewardship over.

Segafriþuz and the Wolf

For many, many days the Widufulka were plagued
by a monster that would come on cold nights and
snatch away the old and young of the tribe.
They lamented their losses, but no one seemed
capable of stopping the beast.
A mighty warrior of the Widufulka, Segafriþuz,
came forward and proclaimed, "I shall kill this
beast!"
The night came and Segafriþuz made a great fire
and stood watch over the Widufulka. As the moon
and stars passed along the sky, the fire grew dim
and Segafriþuz grew tired.
Suddenly he saw a shape in the shadows, but
before mighty Segafriþuz could grab his club a
large wolf leapt from the shadows and snatched up
one of the Widufulka and bounded off into the
woods.

When morning came Segafriþuz told the tribe of what he saw and boldly stated, "The next time I shall be ready for the great wolf!"

Luidibalþaz listened to what Segafriþuz said, then began to cut down trees.

Many more nights passed with nothing happening as Segafriþuz stood guard over the tribe.

Then, after twelve nights, Segafriþuz grew tired and the fire dimmed. The wolf snatched up another of the Widufulka and bounded away.

The tribe lamented and Segafriþuz confidently said, "The wolf shall not take another. I will be ready for the beast this *next* time for certain."

Luidibalþaz listened to what Segafriþuz said, then began fashioning the trees together.

Many more nights passed with nothing happening as Segafriþuz stood guard over the tribe.

Then, after twelve nights, Segafriþuz grew tired and the fire dimmed. The wolf snatched up another of the Widufulka and bounded away.

The tribe lamented and Segafriþuz boldly stated, "I shall defeat the beast this *next* time!"

Luidibalþaz listened to what Segafriþuz said, then covered the trees with bark and mud and moss. He invited the tribe into the husa he made.

The tribe slept within the husa night after night. Then, after twelve nights, the wolf came and pawed and scratched and howled, but could not get to where the Widufulka were sleeping.

He went back into the woods to find other beasts to eat.

The next morning, with none of the tribe taken, Luidibalþaz said, "Sometimes one does better to think, instead of fighting." Segafriþuz was ashamed.

To this day the wolf's children prefer to stay away from the huso that people build.

Luidibalþaz and the Sunthafulka

It was a hard winter and the Widufulka sheltered
in their huso to hide from the cold by their fires
and ate what little food they had saved and that
little food they could find.

Luidibalþaz and Segafriþuz would go out to hunt
for the Widufulka, bringing back what meat they
could chase.

On one cold day Luidibalþaz and Segafriþuz came
upon a group of strange, new fulka coming from
the south. These Sunthafulka carried bags and
baskets on their backs and had all their men,
women, and children with them.

"Please," the Sunthafulka said, "Please help us and
give us shelter. Our homes were burned, our land
taken, and all we have is what we carry."

"I do not trust these Sunthafulka," Segafriþuz said
to Luidibalþaz. "They look strange to my eyes.
They speak strange to my ears."

Luidibalþaz chided his friend, "Who are we if we
turn these Sunthafulka away? If we were cold, our

homes burned, and our lands taken, would we not want them to help us? Would we not be the strange seeming fulka to them?"

Segafriþuz was shamed and hanged his head low. Luidibalþaz and Segafriþuz brought the Sunthafulka to the huso of the Widufulka, and they shared their homes, food, and fires with the Sunthafulka. Half of the Sunthafulka stayed in the husa of Luidibalþaz and half of the Sunthafulka stayed in the husa of Segafriþuz.

The winter was long and cold and after a time the food became scarce. Luidibalþaz and Segafriþuz set out to hunt again, but day after day the game out ran them.

The Sunthafulka began to sing their own songs and tell their own stories to spirits that were stange to the Widufulka. They brought out a great many strange seeds from their bags and baskets and ground them up.

Luidibalþaz and Segafriþuz went out to hunt again and again, but still the game out ran them.

The Sunthafulka melted snow by the fires and mixed the ground up seeds with the water, then baked a great many loaves of brautham by the heat of the fires. They shared this food with the Widufulka.

When Segafriþuz saw the Sunthafulka in his husa doing this he cried out, "Look at these strange fulka with their strange foods amd strange songs! They could not keep their homes and lands, surely we can also easily take these seeds!"

Segafriþuz and his warriors took the seeds from the Sunthafulka in his husa and sent them back out into the cold winter.

"Surely we shall eat well now!" Segafriþuz rejoiced, and he and his warriors ground up all their seeds and made a great many loaves of brautham and were well fed through the rest of winter.

The Sunthafulka that Segafriþuz threw out went to the husa of Luidibalþaz and cried and wept, "Segafriþuz has taken all we had left and sent us out into the cold!"

Luidibalþaz listened to their lamentations then brought them into his husa and shared his fire and food. Luidibalþaz learned their stories and songs and let them make their loaves of brautham, and everyone in his husa ate little during the winter, but no one starved.

When spring came, the Sunthafulka with Luidibalþaz sang new songs and told new stories and planted their remaining seeds in the ground. Spring and Summer passed as they always do for the Widufulka, and the seeds grew into great tall grasses and made many, many new seeds and the Sunthafulka collected them and brought them to their own, new huso amongst the Widufulka.

They brought a great many seeds to Luidibalþaz and exclaimed, "You shared your food and fire with us when we were hungry and cold, now we will share with you!"

The winter that followed was even colder than the last and the game was still faster then Luidibalþaz and Segafriþuz.

When their food was scarce, Segafriþuz lamented, "We will be hungry again, friend!"

Luidibalþaz chided him, "You will be hungry friend. The Sunthafulka you sent out had stories and songs to learn from. Their seeds grew into many more and now they, and I, will have plenty even though the game out runs us. We are always stronger when we learn and share with those different than us, instead of denying and taking from them."

Segafriþuz was ashamed and wept. Luidibalþaz shared his loaves of brautham with Segafriþuz and Segafriþuz listened and learned from the Sunthafulka.

The Herutaz and the Field

In the woods about the Widufulka there lived a great many beasts, but most magnificent amongst them was a great herutaz, a stag of considerable size, whose coat shimmered red and whose antlers stretched out as wide as a man could reach. He was reik of his own herd and he led that herd about the woods boldly, confident of his own speed and strength.

One spring day, the herutaz came upon the Widufulka planting their seeds in a field.

The herutaz exclaimed to his herd, "What strange beasts these are to put seeds and nuts in the ground for me!"

Then one old deer spoke up, "But mighty herutaz, when the seeds and nuts grow these beasts leave us be to roam safely."

The herutaz scoffed, "But there is no beast that can oppose my grace and strength!" He then strode into the field, chased away the Widufulka, and ate their seeds.

Luidibalþaz heard the commotion and approached the herutaz, "Begone! We Widufulka need these seeds and nuts so that we may eat through the winter and leave you be!"

The mighty herutaz ignored Luidibalþaz and dug up all the seeds and left.

Many days later the herutaz returned to find a wall of stone and branches as high as his chest around the field, and the Widufulka were planting seeds again.

The herutaz exclaimed to his herd, "What strange beasts these are to put their seeds and nuts in the ground for me again!"

The old deer spoke up again, "O mighty herutaz, perhaps we should leave these beasts be so that they leave us to ourselves later?"

The herutaz scoffed, "But there is no beast that can oppose my grace and strength!" He then leapt over the wall, chased away the Widufulka, and ate their seeds.

Luidibalþaz heard the commotion and approached the herutaz, "Begone! We Widufulka need these seeds and nuts so that we may eat through the winter and leave you be!"

The mighty herutaz ignored Luidibalþaz and dug up all the seeds and left.

Many days later the herutaz returned to find strange totems of bones and sticks upon the wall, making a clatter when the wind blew threw them, and in the field the Widufulka were planting seeds yet again.

The herutaz exclaimed to his herd, "What strange beasts these are to put their seeds and nuts in the ground for me again!"

The old deer spoke up again, "O mighty herutaz, perhaps we should leave these beasts be; for even small beasts become dangerous when you provoke them again and again."

The herutaz scoffed, "But there is no beast that can oppose my grace and strength!" He then swept the totems aside with his mighty antlers, leapt over the

The herutaz exclaimed to his herd, "What strange beasts these are to put their seeds and nuts in the ground for me again!"

The old deer spoke up again, "O mighty herutaz, perhaps we should leave these beasts be so that they leave us to ourselves later?"

The herutaz scoffed, "But there is no beast that can oppose my grace and strength!" He then leapt over the wall, chased away the Widufulka, and ate their seeds.

Luidibalþaz heard the commotion and approached the herutaz, "Begone! We Widufulka need these seeds and nuts so that we may eat through the winter and leave you be!"

The mighty herutaz ignored Luidibalþaz and dug up all the seeds and left.

Many days later the herutaz returned to find strange totems of bones and sticks upon the wall, making a clatter when the wind blew threw them, and in the field the Widufulka were planting seeds yet again.

The herutaz exclaimed to his herd, "What strange beasts these are to put their seeds and nuts in the ground for me again!"

The old deer spoke up again, "O mighty herutaz, perhaps we should leave these beasts be; for even small beasts become dangerous when you provoke them again and again."

The herutaz scoffed, "But there is no beast that can oppose my grace and strength!" He then swept the totems aside with his mighty antlers, leapt over the wall, chased away the Widufulka, and ate their seeds.

Luidibalþaz and Segafriþuz heard the commotion and approached the herutaz, "Begone! We Widufulka need these seeds and nuts so that we may eat through the winter! We will not warn you again!"

The mighty herutaz ignored Luidibalþaz and Segafriþuz and dug up all the seeds and left.

Many days later the herutaz returned to find the totems and wall gone, and the Widufulka were planting seeds again.

The herutaz exclaimed to his herd, "What strange beasts these are to put their seeds and nuts in the ground for me again!"

The old deer spoke up, "O mighty herutaz, we will not follow you again. You have wronged these beasts too often and I fear what they may do."

The herutaz scoffed, "But there is no beast that can oppose my grace and strength!" He then strode into the field, then Luidibalþaz and Segafriþuz and the Widufulka hunters leapt out from hiding and felled the herutaz with their spears.

Audariks and Haimariks

Amongst the Widufulka lived Audariks and
Haimariks, two brave men and skilled hunters who
were always found together. Neither man took any
wife and neither man sired any children.
The other Widufulka spoke about them in
whispered words but never approached them.
Audariks and Haimariks grew older and built their
own husa, apart from the other huso, and kept to
themselves, mindful of the whispered words about
them.
Audariks and Haimariks came to hunt for the
Widufulka, as the other hunters did.
Audariks and Haimariks came to plant the seeds
with the Widufulka, as the other tribespeople did.
Audariks and Haimariks came and sang the songs
and told the stories as the other Widufulka did,
and prayed to Wodanaz just as the other
Widufulka did.

But always, they returned to their husa alone, surrounded by the whispered words.

One night, when the winds were cold, the fire escaped the hearth in one of the husa and the Widufulka inside had to flee with what few belongings they could carry.

The Widufulka lamented, "What ever shall we do! The night is cold and all we have has been lost!"

They made their way past the husa of Audariks and Haimariks to the husa of Luidibalþaz, and begged that he help them.

Luidibalþaz had seen them pass by the husa of Audariks and Haimariks and he said to them, "I have no room for you! Go to another's husa!"

The Widufulka made their way to the husa of Segafriþuz, again passing by the husa of Audariks and Haimariks.

Segafriþuz had seen them pass by the husa of Audariks and Haimariks and he said to them, "I have no room for you! Go to another's husa!"

The Widufulka lamented, "But where shall we go! We have no place that shall shelter us!"

Segafriþuz replied, "Have you not asked of Audariks and Haimariks?"

The Widufulka recoiled, "But they are strange men with strange ways!"

Segafriþuz burst out with a great fury, "When have they ever failed to come and hunt with the Widufulka? When have they ever failed to come and plant with the Widufulka? When have they ever failed to carry on the songs and stories of the Widufulka? They have never failed to be men of our tribe, while you have done nothing but whispered evil words about them!"

The Widufulka, shamed by Segafriþuz's words, went to the husa of Audariks and Haimariks to beg shelter.

Audariks and Haimariks welcomed them in and shared their hearth and shelter, and shared their food and drink.

The Children and the Fox

When the summer nights cooled, and the wheat ripened, the Widufulka collected their seeds while the children too young to help played. It was at one of these times that Fuhsaz, a fox known among the huso of the Widufulka, saw that the children had left their food unattended.

Fuhsaz said to herself, "Surely the children can spare a meager bite or two of food for all the help I give them!"

So, sly and fast little Fuhsaz crept over to the food and took a portion in her jaws before running back into her woods.

The children saw this and cried out, "Sneaky Fuhsaz! Thieving Fuhsaz!" The children gave chase, but Fuhsaz was too fast and clever for them. The children cried to Luidibalþaz. Luidibalþaz said to them, "Leave her be. She chases away the mice who would eat our seeds. It was a meager bite of food and you shall not go hungry."

On the next day, while the Widufulka collected their seeds and their children played, Fuhsaz came again and saw that they had left their food unattended again.

Fuhsaz said to herself, "Surely the children can spare another meager bite of food since they have enough to leave about!"

So, sly and fast little Fuhsaz crept over to the food and took a portion in her jaws before running back into her woods.

The children saw this and cried out, "Sneaky Fuhsaz! Thieving Fuhsaz!" The children gave chase, but Fuhsaz was too fast and clever for them. The children cried to Luidibalþaz. Luidibalþaz said to them, "Leave her be. She chases away the mice who would eat our seeds. It was a meager bite of food and you shall not go hungry."

On the next day, while the Widufulka collected their seeds, the children had a plan to protect their food and hid.

Fuhsaz came again and saw that they had left their food unattended again.

Fuhsaz said to herself, "Surely the children can spare another meager bite of food since they still have so much to leave about!"

So, sly and fast little Fuhsaz crept over to the food, but before she could take a portion in her jaws the children jumped out with stones and threw them at her.

The children cried out, "Sneaky Fuhsaz! Thieving Fuhsaz!" They pelted the little fox with many stones and gave chase, but Fuhsaz was too fast and clever for them.

For the next twelve days little Fuhsaz did not come to the huso of the Widufulka and the mice carried off a great many seeds.

Luidibalþaz called the children to them and asked of them, "What have you done to little Fuhsaz?"

The children proudly cried out, "We punished the little thief! Our laws say that thieves must be punished!"

Luidibalþaz said to the children, "I want for you to go out into the woods and find little Fuhsaz. Hide and watch her, so that you might find out why she stole."

The children did as Luidibalþaz told them and searched all the woods about the huso until they found a den from which Fuhsaz would come and go.

The children hid and watched as Fuhsaz tended to three small kits, for whom she brought food and trinkets and whom she groomed and cared.

The children returned to Luidibalþaz and said, "Little Fuhsaz had kin for whom she cared."

Luidibalþaz then chided them, "The food she took for her kin, and you had food to spare! She helped us to protect our seeds so that we may eat and only needed help so that she could eat. Our laws say that thieves must be punished, but one should never follow the laws without compassion."

The Albizfulka and the Widufulka

At the end of every winter, when the sun shone hotter and the snows melted away, the Albizfulka, the folk from beyond the otherworld, would emerge in secret to cast about the seeds and sprouts of the wild plants which the animals and Widufulka would harvest.

As the Widufulka grew greater and greater in number, some of the Albizfulka went to their reik, Derkazhert, with concern before the coming of the spring.

They exclaimed, "Our mighty Reik! The Widufulka shall become so great in number that we will run out of seeds and sprouts for all the animals of the woods! What ever shall we do?"

Derkazhert thought and thought, then an idea came to him.

Derkazhert proclaimed, "We shall scare these Widufulka out of the woods!"

When the spring came and the warmth melted the snows, Derkazhert summoned mists into the woods that made strange shadows and silence. This frightened the Widufulka.

They exclaimed, "See how this mist swallows our voices and see the strange beasts in it!"

Luidibalþaz and Segafriþuz were unafraid.

Luidibalþaz calmed them, "See how these mists are nothing more than water and wind, just as my mother and father are."

Luidibalþaz and Segafriþuz walked into the mists and returned unharmed. The Widufulka were calmed and they harvested the wild plants and shoots as they always do.

When the Widufulka still did not leave the woods, more of the Albizfulka went to their reik, Derkazhert.

The Albizfulka exclaimed, "These Widufulka remain! They shall gather more than we can spread!"

Derkazhert thought and thought, then an idea came to him.

Derkazhert proclaimed, "We shall awaken the great beasts of the earth and woods to scare these Widufulka away!"

When the spring came and the warmth melted the snows, Derkazhert blew his mighty horn and awakened bears from caves and hollows, including a great beast named Beranaz.

The Widulfulka had never seen such beasts before and were frightened.

The Widufulka exclaimed, "Look at these mighty beasts! Larger and more fearsome than wolves!"

Luidibalþaz and Segafriþuz were unafraid.

Segafriþuz calmed them, "These are beasts like any other. Let us leave out offerings and let our gathering be guarded by hunters and warriors!

The Widufulka left offerings of food away from their huso and travelled with spears in hand.

Beranaz accepted the offered food and kept his bear children away from the Widufulka who carried spears.

The Widufulka were calmed and they harvested the wild plants and shoots as they always do.

When the Widufulka still did not leave the woods, more of the Albizfulka went to their reik, Derkazhert.

The Albizfulka exclaimed, "These Widufulka remain! They shall gather more than we can spread!"

Derkazhert thought and thought, then an idea came to him.

Derkazhert proclaimed, "We shall mix poisons in with the seeds and shoots."

When the spring came and the warmth melted the snows, the Albizfulka planted the seeds and shoots as always but this time many strange mushrooms and berries sprouted amongst the usual plants.

The Widufulka harvested the wild plants and shoots as they always do, but this time many of the Widufulka became very sick.

Luidibalþaz and Segafriþuz did not know what to do. No matter how much they thought and thought, ideas would not come to them.

Many more Widufulka became sick until an old lady of the Widufulka came to Luidibalþaz and Segafriþuz.

She said, "Many of the plants and fruits and mushrooms that we harvested are strange to me. I have gathered plants since I was young, many twelves of years ago, and never have I become sick like the Widufulka.

Luidibalþaz had an idea and said, "Wise woman, can you teach the younger Widufulka to only gather the plants you remember from those many twelves of years ago."

The old woman taught the Widufulka, and they only gathered that food which they knew was safe from that day on.

Skadwahanduz and the Children

As seasons went on and still the Widufulka
continued to live in the woods, the Albizfulka went
again to their reik, Derkazhert. They said to him,
"These strange folk, these Widufulka, continue to
live in these woods! Make them move away!"
Derkazhert listened to them then thought long
before saying, "Let the most wily of our folk go
and make the Widufulka move!"
The Albizfulka went to their most wily, an
Albizfulka named Skadwahanduz. Skadwahanduz
said, "Let me do my tricks and I will make those
strange folk move away."
He used his tricks and made himself to look like a
Widufulka and went to the woods where the
children of the Widufulka played.
Skadwahanduz used his tricks to make a small
wooden deer appear in his hand and he hid in the

trees and bushes until a small boy of the Widufulka came near.

Skadwashanduz whispered, "Boy, come see this fine toy I have. If you would like to have it you only need come and take it." When the boy took the toy he was taken away by Skadwahanduz's magicks to the land of the Albizfulka.

Skadwahanduz then used his tricks to create a honeyed hearthcake appear in his hand and he hid in the trees and bushes until a small girl of the Widufulka came near.

Skadwahanduz whispered, "Girl, come see this fine treat I have. If you would like to have it you only need come and take it." When the girl took the hearthcake she was taken away by Skadwahanduz's magicks to the land of the Albizfulka.

This happened for many days and Skadwahanduz took many children. The Widufulka grew afraid and they came to Luidibalþaz and Segafriþuz and exclaimed, "We must move away before all of the children are taken away!"

Luidibalþaz and Segafriþuz thought and thought.

The Widulfulka exclaimed again, "We must move away! For if we do not move away all of our children will be taken away!"

Luidibalþaz then said, "But what shall happen when we move away from our herds and our crops, will not our children starve?"

The Widufulka exclaimed, "Our children are being taken now! We must act now!"

Segafrithus then said, "But what shall happen when we move away from our huso? Will not the wild beasts take our children in the night?"

The Widufulka exclaimed, "Our children are being taken now! We must act now!"

Luidibalþaz then said, "Let Segafriþuz and I go to search for the children and what is happening, then we will decide how to act."

Luidibalþaz then disguised himself as a small boy and Segafriþuz himself as a small girl and they went out to the woods where the children of the Widufulka would play.

Skadwahanduz was hiding in the trees and the bushes when Luidibalþaz and Segafriþuz came near. He whispered, "Boy, come see this fine toy I have. If you would like to have it you only need come and take it."

Luidibalþaz replied, "I have no need of your toy."

Skadwahanduz then said, "Girl, come see this fine treat I have. If you would like to have it you only need come and take it."

Segafriþuz replied, "I have no need of your treat."

Skadwahanduz then said, "Boy, what would you like if not this toy?"

Luidibalþaz replied, "I would see your face before I take your hand."

Skadwahanduz then showed his face and held a hand out. He said, "Girl, what would you like if not this treat?"

Segafriþuz replied, "I would know your name before I take your hand."

Skadwahanduz said his name and held out a hand. Luidibalþaz and Seagafrithuz then leaped forth and grabbed Skadwahanduz's arms and exclaimed, "Skadwahanduz, we know you now by hand and face! Give back the children of the Widulfulka!"

Skadwahanduz's magicks were then undone and the children of the Widulfulka were returned. The children of the Widulfulka then knew never to blindly trust the word and gifts of strangers.

Segafriþuz and his Bow

Derkazhert, reik of the Albizfulka had long grown weary of Luidibalþaz and the Widufulka living in the woods. He grew so tired of them that he decided to take all of the Widufulka, once and for all.

Derkazhert gathered all of his warriors and made ready to go after the Widufulka.

Luidibalþaz and Segafriþuz learned of this and gathered all of the Widufulka to speak of it.

Luidibalþaz stood up and said, "I think we should speak to Derkazhert and his Albizfulka, there is no disagreement that we cannot speak through and resolve without conflict."

Segafriþuz had long come to respect the wisdom of Luidibalþaz, but carried his great bow, Ferereikajan, anyway.

The days and nights passed and the Widufulka heard more tales of Derkazhert approaching. They made ready a great feast to welcome him and his Albizfulka and dressed in their finest clothes to speak with him and his fulka.

Segafriþuz joined the Widufulka in readying the feast, but still carried Ferereikajan with him.

The day finally came and the Widufulka greeted the Albizfulka.

Luidibalþaz stood on a hill near all the Widufulkas' huso and spoke out to Derkazhert, "We have readied a great feast for all our fulka so we may talk and resolve our disagreements."

Derkazhert threw a spear at Luidibalþaz, but it missed him.

Luidibalþaz and the Widufulka were stunned, they had greeted Derkazhert and the Albizfulka with nothing but friendliness and hospitality.

Segafriþuz strung Ferereikajan and stood on the hill next to Luidibalþaz. He said, "Friend, it is always good to first greet an enemy with gentleness and friendship, but still be ready if they reject you."

Segafriþuz loosed arrow after arrow upon the Albizfulka while Luidibalþaz led the Widufulka to safety.

Segafriþuz fought on and on and on while his friend escaped until he ran out of arrows and fought Derkazhert with his bare hands. He fought on and on until both he and Derkazhert fell and the Albizfulka fled.

Luidibalþaz and the Widufulka returned in the night and found Segafriþuz fallen on the hill. Luidibalþaz held his friend and wept.

Skeujamann and Saiwif saw their son weeping and Skeujamann carried rain from Saiwif to wash away the tears.

Skeujamann's wind carried the tears up into the sky where they froze, shining among the stars with Segafriþuz's spirit.

To this day Segafriþuz still travels across the night sky with his mighty bow, Ferereikajan, protecting all the fulka below him.

Printed in Great Britain
by Amazon

19375380R00031